CW00434506

The Dream Song of Olaf Åsteson

The Dream Song of Olaf Åsteson

An Ancient Norwegian Folksong of the Holy Nights

Illustrated by Janet Jordan

Floris Books

Illustrated by Janet Jordan

Poem translated by Eleanor Merry

British Library CIP Data available

ISBN 978-086315-620-5

Produced by Polskabook in Poland

Contents

Preface by Jonathan Stedall

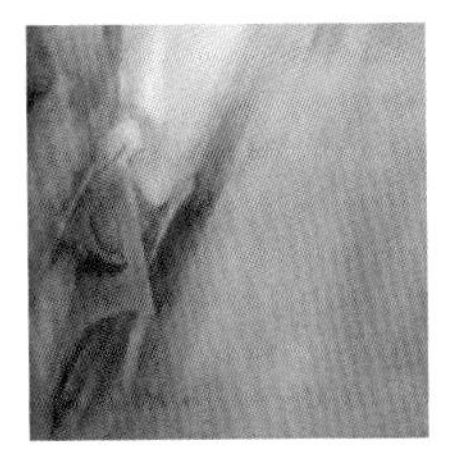

The mystery of sleep has long interested me. We spend about one third of our lives asleep and, apart from those few transitional moments that we call dreams, it seems to be one huge eight-hour blank. The dreams themselves are also, on the whole, a mystery — intimations, perhaps, of truths that our waking consciousness simply cannot grasp or retain.

Sleep, then, is seemingly a time when we have no contact with the world, either through our senses, emotions or intellect. Our bodies continue to tick over, while we take a rest. Or is it, perhaps, more complicated and more meaningful than that? Who are 'we,' and what do we understand by the 'world?'

Any theories depend, of course, on whether or not we sense that the human being is more than their physical body. If there is a reality to the notion of soul and spirit, then it would seem quite possible, and even likely, that this period of sleep is connected with the supersensible aspect of our being reconnecting with those realms out of which it is born and nourished. The fact that we don't remember such experiences is, I believe, merely an indication of the limitations of consciousness at this stage of our evolution, rather than the notion that nothing actually takes place. And the absence of conscious memory doesn't have to mean that we are not influenced and informed by such experiences. Ideas that we have, and initiatives that we take in our daily lives have, as their source, so we tend to believe, our capacity to imagine and to think. But perhaps all sorts of 'voices', both benign and otherwise, are whispering through the windows of our souls while we are sleeping — some clamouring for our attention, others more patient. If so, our capacity not only to listen but also to discriminate — a capacity we are constantly challenged to exercise in our daily lives — is of even greater importance in that time between falling asleep and waking.

The period of sleep that features in this ancient Norwegian poem is what we call the Twelve Holy Nights — that time between Christmas Eve and Epiphany, when the three Wise Men arrive at Bethlehem. Like all festivals, Christmas is as meaningful and enriching as we allow it to be. The degree to which we are open to help and inspiration will influence the extent to which we can be nourished. It is true in daily life, and is, I imagine, even more so in those divine realms and in that eternal dimension from which we originate and in which our existence is rooted.

In the poem, Olaf Åsteson not only has profound experiences related to the mystery of the soul's existence after death, but is also able to remember those experiences and to share them with others. It is what the Initiates of old were able to do, and most religions are based on such revelations. Today, I sense, although there is a seeming silence from those sublime realms, we are challenged in all modesty and humility to gradually tap into that source of wisdom for ourselves. The potential is there, but much work as well as patience is essential. What is also essential is that true illumination will only come about to the extent that we nurture in ourselves the capacity to love, to transcend our egotism, and to care as much about our fellow human beings as we do about ourselves. And it is this message that is for me the essence of what Olaf Åsteson, on his return, tries to share with those assembled in the church on that twelfth day of Christmas. He has slept through all the earthly rituals and celebrations, experiencing for himself those same profound truths now being expressed by the Priest who is 'the Holy Gospel expounding.' And the climax of Olaf's message is contained in the word 'blessed.' Blessed are those who here on earth give shoes, bread, their corn and their clothes to those in need, to the poor. In so doing, reports Olaf Åsteson, we need not fear 'in the other world' all the potentially terrifying trials and experiences that await us on that journey between one life and the next — a journey in which we have to confront the consequences of how we have lived on Earth.

Introduction by Andrew Welburn

I

It is the modern gospel: if something stands in our way, we soon rise to the challenge of overcoming it. If we are building a fast road, we level hills and span valleys; if we face a water-shortage or need electricity, we dam rivers into vast lakes for consumption or for hydroelectric power; if we lack space to live we raise skyscrapers and live stacked in boxes one above another; if we need food that is not in season, we fetch it peremptorily from the other side of the world. If the climate is wet and cold, we still go to work and everything carries on as usual in heated and (perhaps) well insulated offices and factories.

We pride ourselves on this will to shape our own lives, to do what we are determined to do. More questionably, we sometimes suppose that the spirit of titanic determination is coeval with civilization, or even with mankind's 'epic journey.' It is sometimes said that in this spirit human beings built the pyramids despite the lack of engineering machinery, or the Gothic cathedrals while Europe struggled with famine and epidemic. But the truth is that it is actually not so old. Perhaps it goes back in full-blooded form to the Renaissance, or certainly we can see it at a turning-point when we recall the story of the wonderful *duomo* of Florence — Arnolfo di Cambio's ambitious design featuring a huge cupola raised an eyebrow on the town council — for at that time it was not possible to build a dome as large as they proposed; yet they went ahead, in the conviction that by the time the building was sufficiently advanced, the engineering problem would have been solved by the human ingenuity and genius of some future architect! A century later, when the cathedral was largely complete, Brunelleschi's genius proved them right — and his achievement still baffled architects long after his time.

The dome of Florence Cathedral is a wonder to contemplate even today, but the spirit which produced it can have more ambiguous manifestations. In the film *Fitzcarraldo* (1982) Klaus Kinski memorably played a maniacal character determined to transport a ship over a mountain. Its director, Werner Herzog, said that he took the film on because it seemed to him that it was a tremendous metaphor — though for what, he was not very sure. But that is precisely the point. The drive to overcome every obstacle, to do the seemingly unachievable, *is* the meaning, not the specific thing that is achieved thereby. The film raises the question of where this potent drive in human civilization leads us, and acknowledges both its power and its irrational aspects.

It did used to be thought that the pyramids of Egypt were built by the use of massive slave labour. Perhaps fuelled by Hollywood images, we readily picture the drudging slaves sweating and dying in order to achieve the superhuman scale of the monument demanded by the tyrannical Pharaoh, lashed on by pitiless overseers under the equally pitiless sun. Yet the growth of understanding and our (still limited) information about the building of the pyramids has actually revealed the opposite. Accounts and depictions of the scene reveal small numbers of specialist workers, who must have possessed greater knowledge of building techniques than we can, as yet, actually reconstruct today. Evidently, rather than being imposed upon nature by sheer human might, a subtle understanding and responsiveness to the forces involved somehow enabled these extraordinary monuments to be raised. The Egyptians saw the pyramidal form as 'shining down' upon the earth, not brutally raised up from it. Ideas that the power of the sun's energy itself was focused to shape the stone have so far proved impossible to prove. But the Egyptians, there as everywhere else, certainly felt their constructions to be *in harmony* with the world they were changing, not forced upon it. Their colossal statues grow out of cliff faces; the temples grow inwardly from columns shaped as the papyrus plants of the mythic primal swamp; and in death the Pharaohs, like their divine prototype Osiris, become one with the landscape and with the patterns of natural order which sustain it — and also sustain the people who inhabit it. He is, among many other things, present in the water of the Nile which periodically brings the soil to such abundant life. Perhaps the gentle but amazing power of the river is the model for the creative powers used by the Egyptians.

One has only to visit Egypt to realize that the Nile and its fecund valley are the focus of life for human beings, animals and plants and birds alike. All must share its resources. The Egyptian images of animal, human and bird-deities suddenly cease to be strange. They are the blindingly obvious truth of life there. So fascinated have we become with human achievement, with stamping our own impress upon the world, that we easily miss the special quality which attached to older civilizations; that of becoming at one with the forces that worked around and through the humanly-fashioned world. Anthropologists have come to grasp what earlier investigators of early man were far too inclined to see, for instance, signs of 'man the mighty hunter.' The progress of human evolution was not made one-sidedly by overcoming and taking what we need from the environment. Many of the prehistoric tools once thought to be weapons of the huntsman are now understood as carving and sharing implements, suggesting a way of life that promoted giving and transforming, not just overcoming and dominating. Moreover, study of surviving archaic cultures shows that hunting itself was by no means just about human supremacy over other species. The Bushman who stalks his prey, unaided except for his spear, must track the animal often through difficult country, following subtle indications of its flight, mentally putting himself into its instinctive responses, anticipating its every move, running with it until, exhausted, it finally gives in to the hunter. And in that moment when he has most deeply shared in every motion and instinct of its being, he kills it with a prayer — more like a deeply moving sacrifice than prey to his superior might.

In the course of modern history, especially since the Renaissance, we have come to experience *ourselves* with unprecedented intensity — exploring our potential and creative resources. Science too belongs to this phase of our evolution, since it seeks the kind of knowledge which gives us the ability to control, to manipulate the world around us. Mediaeval people, as C.S. Lewis once pointed out, had a much more hands-on knowledge of biology and especially zoology than we can readily imagine, for they lived with animals breeding in their yards and fields, if not in their own houses, and were dependent on the management of plants and crops for their day-to-day existence. Yet we find it baffling that their accounts of zoology are full of unicorns and pelicans performing emblematic gestures, where greyhounds 'figure' the resurrection as lions do the kingship of England, and the iconic inhabitants of their bestiaries stare out at us with eyes of mystical resonance rather than practical familiarity. What has become of all that intimate animal knowledge in their day-to-day lives? To find the answer, we need only consider, however, that for all its intimacy their relationship to the natural world was still largely one of admiring dependency, not of exploitation. The kind of knowledge they had was not of the sort that implies wide-scale control, but co-dependency on the seasonal and natural cycles. Therefore, they quite rightly found in animals and trees signs of the unchanging 'divine' order, of the generosity of natural world, moral emblems of selfless love in the pelican, of the dependence of society on the order of nature in the lion. Their emblems told them 'scientifically' and accurately about the close relationship of their society to the natural world with which it still significantly overlapped. Later, Darwin would present knowledge of nature in terms of the Victorians' attempt to harness resources for industry and commerce, a competitive order in which species are successes or failures, and in which a 'struggle for survival' went on which explicitly took up Malthus' statistical approach to human populations as the subject for analysis and regulation. To the Victorians both civilization and nature were seen as competitors, as they have remained ever since, and so the whole of knowledge must be reconceived in competitive terms.

By developing manipulative knowledge, especially in modern science, we have learned how to win the competition into which we engaged ourselves — to win it to a staggering extent as detailed in those engineering feats, skyscrapers, power stations, dams, and so on from which we began. Undoubtedly, we have learned a 'truth' about the world in the process, and perhaps still more importantly we have learned to intensify our own self-experience; though on the whole we understand that, in its deeper ramifications, rather less. We have not very clearly learned, perhaps, that this kind of knowledge, which sets us in competition with nature, has its origins in our own powerful inner drives as well as in the world we come to know. Nor have we been quick to realize that this kind of knowledge is not the only kind of knowledge, nor even always the most important sort of knowledge that is available — or that is needed for the wider solution of the problems which arise, and arise, it seems, precisely through the one-sided development whose huge and dramatic consequences, ecological and social, we are now witnessing.

There is a kind of modern myth, especially pervasive since the eighteenth-century Enlightenment, which says not only that our view is best, but that it is also the only one which matters. Everything that came before was just superstition, or at best a confused pioneering attempt to be as we are today. Now, let us by all means value the achievements and the special insights of modernity. But it may be that historical awareness in a deeper sense, which is also a specifically modern achievement, is necessary if we are really to understand how we got here, and how to relate peaceably to other peoples who have taken somewhat different routes.

II

Rudolf Steiner was a twentieth-century Austrian philosopher and esotericist who tried to bring such a deeper understanding to modern civilization. He was not trying to hold modernity back from the path it had chosen — indeed, he was drawn to the philosophies of those such as Nietzsche who were blazing its trail, and elaborated his own version of the Phenomenology which was trying to define more clearly the philosophical basis of the sciences. But his deepest concern, as he surveyed modernity's direction and achievements, was for the 'dehumanization' he foresaw as the danger in our own age, and he sought to bring to modern knowledge an enriched awareness of its own history and, thereby, also its implications for the future. That was at least a major part of what he called Anthroposophy, a 'wisdom of our humanity.'

He tried to place our modern perspective on things, valid in its own terms, within an 'evolution of consciousness' that would enable us to understand our relationship to other ways of seeing. Though sometimes misunderstood, his intention was not at all to go back to previous ideas — or to foster 'alternative' ones — but fundamentally to deepen and extend the knowledge and attitude of consciousness we have come to evolve, so that we might be able to shape its future direction with greater insight. Modern consciousness, as he said, must become apocalyptic; a vision of the future. For as we have seen, the modern scientific drive to master the cosmos is intensely rational and conscious in some ways, yet driven by powerful half-conscious forces in others. Science has nothing to fear from admitting that scientists are human. Scientists were just as naive as anyone else in thinking that the space race was motivated by the desire to make a giant leap for mankind, but discovered that substantial funding for it was a symptom of Cold War rivalries. Richard Dawkins can proudly claim that Darwinism is actually seen to work in the economics of big business. But, if we only manage to see through the Alice-in-Wonderland looking-glass of our surface awareness to become critically aware of our thinking, a little reflection will suggest that Darwinism's ideas were, in reality, taken over from Victorian capitalism in the first place.

Rudolf Steiner's goal in his philosophical, and later anthroposophical, work is to make us aware of our thinking, in this sense, not to catch us out but to reveal it as a creative element. (Steiner's basic book of ideas is his *Philosophy of Freedom.)* If we have eyes fixed only on the object of our thought, we cannot be free in relation to it. We may discover powerful aspects of the truth, yet we may be driven by them to carry our ship over the mountain. But if we understand what has shaped our changing relationship to the world around us, and that our ideas also express our own stage of awareness, we can be freely creative in our inner life rather than driven. So in asking us to make the experiment of comprehending what it meant to think and feel in other, often older ways, and get to know them *from the inside* (so far as we can), his aim was essentially to help us on the trajectory we ourselves are travelling, and to see the fuller potential of the human. When we have gone our way of modernity, and shaped our future, we may indeed still need all that we have gained in empathy and the ability to get outside our immediate situation, to cope with what we find! Modern knowledge may be something we need to use, not only to serve; and older knowledge may also tell us something of what its human purposes may be. We need the sense of the whole trajectory, from that older consciousness of belonging, through the stage of detached objective knowledge which yet imperils our own inner balance, through to ... well, that is the future we must envision on the basis of the largest map we can devise of our human situation.

Suppose we make his experiment. This book with its old Norwegian folk poem, perhaps it may seem surprising to say, is one which can help us to undertake just that. And if we do, it is a book whose content can also become an imaginative possession not just for illuminating the past but, if taken in Steiner's 'anthroposophical' sense, for shining a light upon our future too.

We are so used to projecting our own attitudes back onto our ancestors. Our central heating, thermal insulation, even cars warmed by circulated air, keep us immune from winter's chill. So we tend to imagine that our unfortunate ancestors in archaic times, who did not have these luxurious technologies at their disposal, would have concentrated upon keeping warm through the winter months, perhaps huddling around fires or keeping close in caves. Of course, everyone needs to stay warm to survive, at least in northern climes, but that was not the uppermost thought in the ancients' way of looking at things. They did not try to shut the cold out, pretending it did not exist, or imagining themselves on the Costa del Sol; those things, as we have just mentioned, were anyway not possible and the winter cold was something which no one could really escape. Indeed winter remained often fatally formidable, especially to the old and young, until relatively recent times. Yet neither, however strangely it sounds to us initially, did older generations try to run away from the experience. A character in Shakespeare remarks that 'A sad tale's best for winter,' and if anything, the ancients actually tried to be wintry in winter; to feel its freezing, life-threatening power and dramatize it in human terms.

If we go back to the ancient Greeks, we find that so far from trying to evade the experience, the tellers of myths and stories gave a wonderfully articulate expression to a still stronger wish — to empathize, to become one with winter. No culture has loved life more than that of the Greeks; yet they sat around their fires in winter (if we suppose they did) telling not escapist stories but one of the most powerful myths of all time. As they drew imaginative life out of the experience of winter, with its seemingly dead earth, barren of life and greenery, they found themselves sensing at once a profound presence — a great-souled Mother Earth, and the pangs of the most terrible grief she was feeling for her child. They did not wish the experience of winter-deprivation away but humanized it, as they tried to find an adequate story to express what nature was saying with their whole soul. In their souls they deepened the pain of the inert, cold face of nature into the brooding grief of the Earth-Mother, Ge-meter or De-meter, pining for her child Persephone.

Therefore, What to us is 'outer nature' became to them, at the same time, an intensity that they felt within themselves, in the deepest way human beings can feel. Instead of positioning themselves inwardly against nature, sheltering their own selves, as it were from distress, the storytellers of ancient Greece allowed nature to speak through them; the course of the seasons became the story of Demeter and Persephone, who returns to the living world with the spring. But it is not a 'nature myth' as used to be asserted. It did not mean to tell about the seasons. In fact, in the story people did not encounter a set of pictures *about* nature, but the gods of nature actually lived the story. They were telling it through human speakers, just as Homer claims.

If people did yearn for the new life of spring as they told the winter-story, therefore, it was not because they were yearning for something that now was not. In Greek culture this mood rather became the artistic form *tragedy*, which does not offer a happy ending. Resolution came rather because by this method of empathizing so strongly with nature, they also knew at the same time the reality of the other half of the story —Persephone's rescue and her return to the upper air from the Underworld of death. The hidden life-within-death was not a hope or an abstract wish, but a definite presence all along, Persephone underground, even while the great Mother was in outer nature searching for her in vain through the earthly, wintry world. This is what we mean by the timelessness of myth, even though it has a story to tell. And through being myth, nature had an inner side; human ideas, images or stories were not abstractions, but also shared directly in the truth of nature, in accordance with what anthropologists have sometimes called a *participation mystique* that is typical for early cultures. Rudolf Steiner's follower Owen Barfield has likewise spoken in marvellous depth about the 'participating' consciousness which historically preceded our own, when ideas or explanations did not feel 'made up,' but were perceived almost in the same way as outer things.

The great and characteristic achievements of ancient culture — in society, the arts, architecture and even sport — were thus founded on their remarkable ability to be in harmony with the world around them, inwardly as well as outwardly: quite the opposite of our own dominant mode of awareness. Games like the famous Olympics were competitive, but they were also a way of showing that human activity was open, at least at moments, to the presence of the gods. The triumphant winners at the festivals were celebrated by great poets such as Pindar — see his wonderful *Odes* for the ancient Olympic and other games — because in their moment of victory they showed that there was something divine, heroic, working in human nature and bursting through: the poet would then naturally recall the legends about their noble ancestors or actual descent from the gods. At that instant no one could doubt it! For that moment they transcended the merely human condition and touched that of the gods, though human beings could not expect to remain on that exalted level. 'Running one's race' became the favoured metaphor in Greek culture for the course of human life itself.

Physical exhilaration and spiritual uplift are here at one. But in a more profound sense there were individuals who had made the divine, or inner side of the world, a humanly articulate truth — who lived it more fully and permanently so that through their lives or their experiences and insights they established patterns for human contemplation and enabled them to be told in story and myth. In later times people might do that in a personal, individual way to suit our modern world, but ancient heroes performed more archetypal deeds. In ancient times people rather sank their personality into the greater truth that was the setting of many people or a whole society, or even of the greater world which shaped their way of life. Though it is hard to fathom their meaning in detail, the 'Mysteries' of the ancient world were solemn religious practices which enabled a small number of the gifted to live the myths in some total sense, fusing their own experience with that of the divine happenings. Those who took part in them were called 'Initiates.' They were regarded as the source of all knowledge, and in the earliest times directed much of the day-to-life of the whole community by their wisdom. If myths and rites were a way in which many people continued to find the presence of the gods, the Initiates went further and in a mystic sense actually *became* the god. At the religious centre of Eleusis, near Athens, the Initiates experienced directly what it meant to be a lost child of the divine Mother, to go down to death — and also to win through once more to rebirth, to god-like life. Or to put it another way: it was their infinitely deep experiences in the Mysteries which, from ancient times, enabled them to put into symbol and story the hopes, convictions and values which spread out into, and informed, the ancient civilizations. They gave meaning to the natural cycle (as we would call it) of winter and summer, death and life, by revealing in human terms its inner truth. It became a way of describing the intuitions of the soul — something that has so largely evaporated from the bleak modern world.

If we were to go back still further, we should find societies which were still more directly dependent on the truth brought back from such extraordinary encounters with the 'other side,' the hidden dimension of life. The older Greek heroes, such as Jason, journey to the realms beyond the edge of the world (later domiciled in geography, or approximately so at least). They passed through the initiatory ordeals (the Clashing Rocks, the Dragon's Teeth), which show that they have within them the heroic spark of the divine, and bring back the ultimate prize, but only when aided by the magic other soul which is their higher self, as we should say nowadays. Jason is aided by Medea, who has such magic powers. The wonderful bard Orpheus, we remember, also journeyed down to the realm of the dead to bring back his lost companion Eurydice — though in this case he failed, and has only the consolation of inspired song; a paradigm, perhaps, for the culture of later times.

In Greece, the old inspiration lived on in art, and the ancient wisdom became more intellectual, philosophical wisdom. But if we were to look among the survivals of archaic cultures among the surrounding countries over the centuries, we should still find many traces of the ancient patterns. The Initiate's journey to the other world to find the wholeness of existence, both life and death, persisted often in debased forms as shamanism — and since the great work of Mircea Eliade there is widespread recognition among scholars that modern shamans are a remnant of an old 'high religion' from Central Asia; a religion of the sky-Father, earth-Mother and of the divinity of the animals, such as we find too in the oldest traces of Indian culture. In Iran, there survived the very ancient religion of Zarathustra, known as Zoroastrianism, which nurtured elements of the magic journey and perhaps contributed to the symbolism of that greatest and most evocative of all subsequent quests, which now became in mediaeval Christian form the Quest for the Holy Grail. And certainly there we find accounts of the initiatory journey. When the knowledge of the spiritual world grows dim with time, the young Arda Viraz (or Viraf) is said to have been chosen to undertake it. After rituals of preparation and purification, the young man lies down and his soul leaves his body: over three days he is shown the wonders of heaven and hell. It is not really hell in our sense, however, since Zoroastrianism preserves that archaic conviction of which we spoke above, that life will always come through, triumphing even over death. Even the worst sins cannot drag us down forever or extinguish our spark of good. Nevertheless, the forces of death are real, if temporary, and have to be overcome on the soul's journey. But to this extent the account differs from the *Divine Comedy* of Christendom's greatest poet, Dante Alighieri, which it probably helped to inspire.

Modern Western scholars are naturally very interested in the psychology of religions, and the mystic journey offers a good deal to psychological reflection. But we should also realize that this is not at all what would have struck an older humanity in the times when the journey was still undertaken. Much more significant, in their eyes, would have been the fact that the journey cannot be undertaken just when it suits our own soul, but must be co-ordinated with certain special conditions and certain definite times — something we moderns find hard to understand. Eliade for instance notes that alignment with cosmic events and relationships is indeed typical for archaic consciousness, but does so as if in a puzzled, questioning 'aside.' Only if we realize that consciousness was really different in ancient phases of humanity's evolution, when these practices originated, can we make sense of it. For we will realize then that the motive-power for these journeys into the spiritual dimension of things was not the personal will of an individual. It was the cosmic forces themselves which took the seer on his journey. We have come to act so much out of ourselves that we find this hard to comprehend. But the mystic journey was not about one's personal search for God, as it is for us; it was the ability to harmonize with the inner aspect of life, and to be transported by the forces that were at work at certain moments of cosmic balance — turning-points, for instance, in the cycle of the year. Later abstractions of 'grace' succeed to the vivid impression we get in the old apocalyptic writings (such as the *Book of Enoch*) where the seer is taken into heaven by an angel, who also explains all that is happening. Somewhere in-between is Dante's sense of being guided by a definite and effective figure who embodies God's grace — either the poet Virgil who guides him through the lower regions, or his equivalent to the female higher-self from the World Beyond, his beatified love, Beatrice.

III

All this may seem to be opening vistas that are rather grand and remote, and the reader may be wondering what they have to do with the folk poem material of this book, which presents in artistic form the *Dream of Olaf Åsteson.* This little work is not known among the great masterpieces of world-poetry and literature. It will be utterly unfamiliar, no doubt, to most — unless they belong to the few who have had occasion to delve into Norwegian folk poetry! But the remarkable material which we encounter there is rooted in those huge vistas of the past — which means that in Steiner's evolutionary sense it must also tell us something about our present and future.

'This poem only came to light about 1850,' explains Eleanor Merry in the foreword to her translation. 'A clergyman named Landstad, who was interested in such things, discovered it in a lonely valley in Telemark. How long it had existed, no one seems to know ...' That is in the nature of folk poetry, which is not usually written down at all but taught from generation to generation to those who will treasure it. By this means bardic material can be transmitted essentially unchanged over long periods of time, especially when it is associated with musical form. The traditional Norwegian melodies (reproduced in and appendix to Eleanor Merry's translation) consist of several 'modes,' to be used as appropriate in the several parts of the poem.

The strange and cryptic narrative tells how a young man, Olaf Åsteson, slept for twelve nights in the depths of winter, and then awoke to tell of the wondrous sights he had seen when his soul left its body. He travelled in the sky, and in the depths of the sea; he saw the cosmic ice fields; and he crossed the perilous Gjaller Bridge which separates this world from the other world, guarded by the fierce triad of Serpent, Hound and Bull. Turning then to the right-hand path he glimpsed the Paradise of the Blest. But he was also shown the terrible Judgment, and the punishment of evil witches and sinners. As his vision unfolds, the forces of Darkness assume cosmic dimensions, for he sees them riding 'out of the north,' to be encountered by the armies of Light. The powers which stir human beings to deeds, good or ill, are also forces that are warring in the cosmos — destruction, perversity, death *versus* life, affirmation, generosity. Moral life is not about personal intentions, but about participating in the elemental forces of cosmic life itself – or, by failing to fulfil them, we are setting ourselves in denial of their gifts. Winter is the near-triumph of the coldness of this anti-life. The life-denying powers come riding out of the frozen polar regions of the north, but they are met and rebuffed by the forces of light, warmth and life from the south. For we are at the very turning-point of the year around the winter solstice, when at last the dark and cold has reached its farthest incursion and begins to recede before the lengthening of the days and the daily higher course of the sun.

Olaf has experienced this as both natural and spiritual reality. He has won through to a vision of human renewal, passed through the Judgment — by sharing in the great struggle to turn the year around over those central twelve days: there is a magical suspension of the so nearly-victorious cold and dark, and after its terrible ebb the return of life flows ever more strongly. Rudolf Steiner spoke with his customary insight about the fact that Olaf is in this way 'initiated, as it were, by the very powers of nature.' (Rudolf Steiner's remarks are to be found especially in his lectures *The Birth of the Sun Spirit* and *Olaf Åsteson — The Awakening of the Earth-Spirit.)* Olaf is carried in his visionary state of consciousness on a strange steed — an embodiment of nature-forces that transports him into the cosmos and brings him back again to his body. The triumph of the light is a renewal of the sun's life-giving power, the turning-point of the seasons. The earth now will awaken to life once more. But through Olaf the process gains a higher dimension of meaning. It is intensified to the level of human existence, and lends strength to Olaf by showing him the eternal aspect of humanity. Thereby the human struggle between darkness and light can be resolved for us, even while we are here below in the transient world, since the ultimate fates of those on each side have been revealed.

From the outset, Janet Jordan's paintings are of wonderful value to us here. Whereas many might expect to find in an artistic treatment a sequence of vivid scenes suggested by such a poem, she has reached deeper for her inspiration. For around Olaf and his unusual animal-mount we immediately feel not just external impressions but an inner moving power. She has been able to make us sense intuitively the revolution of great natural and spiritual cycles. And as a result she has also shown the profound unity of imagination behind the poem. Everything arises out of the inner working and balance of forces.

In order to become the bearer of that knowledge on the human level, Olaf must indeed be able to undergo a profound process of inner change and transformation. For to cross the Gjaller Bridge means nothing less than to die to existence in this world. It is a part of that symbolism of threshold and changing spiritual perspective which is at the heart of the ancient traditions of enlightenment. Many shamans and seers describe how they cross such a bridge over 'nothingness,' 'the Void outside of existence' — in other words, it is the bridge between one condition of being and another, so that everything we were must cease to be, and on the other side of that nothingness, if we can, we may grasp hold of a new, cosmic identity. Those who are inwardly ready can make the transition; those who are not prepared risk losing all that they are in that void. In the Zoroastrian traditions which still echo these experiences, the 'Bridge of the Separator' straddles the void on the path to the higher worlds; for those who are suited to that higher existence, it seems that there is a broad way over the abyss, but for those who are unripe or morally unfit, the broad way shrinks to the width of a razor's edge, they wobble and fall into the pit. The beasts, which Olaf encounters at the crossing, are therefore in one way aspects of himself — the aspects which are not yet fully spiritualized, and prevent his crossing over. Rudolf Steiner too, in the images he carved into the coloured glass windows of the Goetheanum building in Switzerland, showed these beasts, which we have to conquer on the path to higher worlds. And often he referred under various aspects to the 'Guardian' who stands at the threshold, preventing us from farther advance until we are able to face our bestial self and transform it.

Olaf undergoes then, as Steiner says, an initiation. Through his self-overcoming he is able to open himself to forces beyond himself; cosmic forces that transport him on his mystical journey like a magic steed. The recurring description of these heavenly 'pathways' into the Beyond is vividly shamanic:

> The Moon shone bright
> And the paths were far to follow.

Everything conspires to suggest that the folk tradition, which preserved the *Dream-Song of Olaf Åsteson,* was a genuine continuation of old mystical and shamanic traditions in the north. The one 'chosen' to have such an experience was shown the cosmic secrets so that he could tell them again to a community, as does Olaf. The renewal of human culture lies on the same plane as the renewal of the world each spring, or of the cyclic 'world-ages' that are spoken of in all the old traditions, according to which even the order of the gods must fade and be reborn from time to time. How different are the implications of all this from the modern projection-back of our own attitudes, which sees the pyramids or the great Homeric epics as monuments of human self-assertion! Here all depends on the selflessness which can make someone a vehicle of greater, cosmic powers and intuit their meaning for his own time and culture.

The Christian elements are few, and some of them are only on the surface. It is natural that a mediaeval reciter would have thought of seeing the Mother of God in Paradise. Was there originally a goddess such as the archaic Mistress of the Animals, or a more sophisticated representation like the Zoroastrian's *Daena* or *Den,* at once a personification of their Religion and, mysteriously, to each individual his own higher self? Each one who crosses the Bridge of the Separator meets her as a beautiful mirror-image of him- or herself, the embodiment of his own religiously motivated 'good deeds,' or as the ugliness of his own wrongdoing. But there are more profound implications when we find Christ and the archangel Michaël as leaders of the forces of the Light, who gain the upper hand as the New Year — or the cosmic New Year — begins. For this suggests that Christianity can keep us in touch with something of the old cosmic wisdom, while also meeting more modern needs. Indeed, it seems that the coming of Christianity is being portrayed here as that renewal of spirituality for the new world-cycle. The twelve 'Holy Nights' of Christmas are a reminder of the cosmic truth behind the birth of the Christ-child on earth.

Paradoxically, perhaps, we may still tend to be too mediaeval in our attitude to Christianity. The great scholastic thinkers brought Christian thinking to perfection, in a certain way at least. And for them anything that was not 'pure' Christianity was therefore diabolic, heresy or worse. But that was not the attitude which had allowed Christianity to enter into, and shape, the life of the whole of Europe, or to play a part in the evolution of modern spiritual life. And what Rudolf Steiner meant by Christianity was not a set of dogmatic ideas, but a living force for inner change — the 'Christ-impulse', as he called it, corresponding to that 'divine-human energy of Christ' which was still spoken of in the old Orthodox theology. Christianity did not reach pagan Europe and take root there as a new system of dogmatic thought, but was understood in many diverse ways and particularly from the background of the old Mysteries, still echoed in a work like the *Dream-Song.* Rudolf Steiner argued, and many more recent discoveries have tended to prove him right, that Christianity was from the outset in touch with the Mysteries of the ancient world. From the Bible it also took something of that idea of individual salvation which had been nurtured in Israel. First a special 'people of God,' and then later individuals like the prophets could form a special link to God. Christianity deepened that idea further — but it at the same time kept it in touch with the cosmic drama which is still so wonderfully vivid in the Book of Revelation, for instance. Interpretation has become so one-sided that such 'visions' and revelations are assumed to have only personal significance. We find it startling even to think otherwise; but the truth is that they are visions like those of the Mysteries, whose meaning is the renewal of society through the rhythms of time and through being in touch with cosmic forces. A John or an Olaf – both are significant not just in themselves, but for being able to register a profound cosmic moment and its potential.

In its humble, folklore aspect, the *Dream-Song of Olaf Åsteson* speaks to us with natural authenticity. Yet it touches on matters that also take us to the heart of great religious documents and the nature of human existence. Anthroposophy does not ask us to go back to times when human life could be determined by the rhythms of nature and the spirit in nature. But it does suggest that we can learn something more than timely from an awareness of the different consciousness out of which ancient myths and poetry spoke. Rudolf Steiner's *Calendar of the Soul* is intended to let us experience again the inner meaning of the yearly cycle, though in a free way that encourages us to be aware not just of the current moment, but also its polar opposites, or the half-way stages between the turning-points, so that we always have within ourselves the resources of the whole. Yet we can work with the quality of the time, and share its special gifts even though we are never just of the moment. It is profoundly Christian, but especially in the understanding of how older Mysteries or winter rebirth became Christmas celebration, spring life-out-of-death became the Mystery of Easter. Another way is that of artistic work; always our own in its creative uniqueness, art is the way we also acknowledge the enrichment that comes through outer senses and spirit in rich interplay. There too we can be free and ourselves, while we respond to the values and insights of others — or other civilizations. Janet Jordan's work beautifully aids us in distinguishing the living, inwardly transforming power of this old saga from its archaic language. Her paintings give modern expression to its lesson of selfless working with the creative forces that we still need — or more than ever — to renew modern life.

Sources

Merry, Eleanor — *The Dream Song of Olaf Åsteson*

Steiner, Rudolf — *The Birth of the Sun Spirit* (Hanover 1911)
Olaf Åsteson — The Awakening of the Earth-Spirit (Berlin 1911)

Further Reading

Steiner, Rudolf — *Christianity as Mystical Fact*
The Evolution of Consciousness
The Cycle of the Year as Breathing Process of the Earth
Calendar of the Soul

Welburn, A (ed) — *The Mysteries: Rudolf Steiner's Writings on Spiritual Initiation*

Barfield, Owen — *Saving the Appearances: A Study in Idolatry*

Eliade, Mircea — *Shamanism*
Myths, Dreams and Mysteries

Halifax, Joan — *Shamanic Voices*

Vahman, Fereydun — *Arda Viraz Namag: The Iranian 'Divine Comedy'*

The Dream Song of Olaf Åsteson

Come listen to me and hear my song
The song of a wondrous youth,
I'll sing of Olaf Åsteson
Who slept many days — 'tis the truth.
Yes, it was Olaf Åsteson
Who lay so long a-sleeping.

It was Christmas Eve when down he lay
And slept so long all unknowing,
He never woke till the thirteenth day
When to Church the people were going.
Yes, it was Olaf Åsteson
Who lay so long a-sleeping.

'Twas the Holy Night when down he lay
Such wonders seeing and hearing
And wakened not till the thirteenth day
When the drowsy birds were stirring.
Yes, it was Olaf Åsteson
Who lay so long a-sleeping.

1. The heavy form of Olaf Åsteson, found in sleep, dreams, as the rider, the crossing over from day-time consciousness to the supersensible worlds.

He never woke till the thirteenth day
When the Sun came up at dawning,
Then he saddled his horse and rode away
To ride to Church in the morning.
Yes, it was Olaf Åsteson
Who lay so long a-sleeping.

The Priest he stood at the altar there
The Holy Gospel expounding,
While Olaf sat down at the outer door
And told of his visions astounding.
Yes, it was Olaf Åsteson
Who lay so long a-sleeping.

The aged men and the younger ones two —
His tale for a past-time taking —
Hear Olaf Åsteson tell them true
His Dream-filled sleep and awakening
Yes, it was Olaf Åsteson
Who lay so long a-sleeping.

I laid me down on this Christmas night,
In sleep profound and unending,
And wakened not till the thirteenth day
When all to the Church were wending.
The Moon shone bright
And the paths were far to follow.

I wandered far, above the cloudy wrack,
In depths of the ocean after —
But he who travels along my track
On his lips there will never be laughter.
The Moon shone bright
And the paths were far to follow.

I wandered above in cloudy height
And plunged in bottomless waters,
And depths of Hell have burned in my sight,
I've glimpsed the heavenly pastures.
The moon shone bright
And the paths were far to follow.

And I have forded the holy stream
And through the deep valleys going
I heard the waters and saw them not —
Beneath the Earth they were flowing.
The Moon shone bright
And the paths were far to follow.

Never a whinny came from my horse
Never a cry from my houndling,
Nor any note of a singing bird
Such wonders there were abounding.
The Moon shone bright
And the paths were far to follow.

At first my sense was ravished away,
I fed through the thorny moorland,
My scarlet mantle was torn away,
The nails of my feet were wounded.
The Moon shone bright
And the paths were far to follow.

2. This first trial experience depicts the four primeval elements of Earth, Air, Fire and Water. These manifest themselves as a gigantic vortex. Despite the strength of their combined essences, Olaf Åsteson maintains his individuality.

O then I came to the Gjaller Bridge
So high in the winds suspended,
And all with gold were its beams bedecked
And spikes with its rafters blended.
The Moon shone bright
And the paths were far to follow.

The serpent strikes, and savage the hound,
In the middle lies the traverse,
Three dread things on the Gjaller mound —
And all are crooked and monstrous.
The Moon shone bright
And the paths were far to follow.

The serpent strikes and the fierce hound bites,
The bull stands ready to ram me —
None will pass over the Gjaller heights
Who with judgment false have damned.
The Moon shone bright
And the paths were far to follow.

3. Olaf Åsteson approaches the Gjaller Bridge of Light. He is confronted by three beasts. He asks if he is worthy to meet the challenge of crossing a threshold whereby a new power is given for man to understand and conquer his animal nature. Those who have failed are shown in the shadows beneath.

But I have crossed over the Gjaller Bridge
    Stern passage so grim and olden,
Have waded through mournful swamps and sedge
    And now I am free and unholden.
        The Moon shone bright
        And the paths were far to follow.

Waded have I through mire of despair
    My pathways were never on earth,
And thus did I climb the Gjaller stair
    With the dust of death in my mouth.
        The Moon shone bright
        And the paths were far to follow.

And then I came where the waters part
    From fiery blue to burning ice,
But God did put it into my heart
    To pass, and turn away mine eyes.
        The Moon shone bright
        And the paths were far to follow.

4. Olaf is confronted by the icy waste, but is allowed to pass.

I went my way by the winter road
    Which turned aside at my right hand,
Faint glimpses of Paradise it showed
    And a light lay over the land.
        The Moon shone bright
        And the paths were far to follow.

God's Holy Mother did I see there —
    O nothing better could befall! —
"Now go on thy way to Brokksvalin
    Thy way unto the Judgment Hall."
        In Brokksvalin
        Shall the Judgement be.

There was I in that other world
    Through many nights and long,
And God in Heaven knoweth well
    What fearful things among.
        In Brokksvalin
        Shall the Judgment be.

5. From the starry realms, Olaf observes a man carrying the burden of a child he has murdered and above them in Paradise, the radiant figure of his Christian godmother. The strong central vortex expresses the renewal of the impulse to go forward into higher worlds.

And there I met a wicked man
The first that I did see —
A little boy was in his arms
He waded to the knee.
In Courts of Pain
Shall the Judgment be.

And when I came up close to him.
His mantle was of lead,
For in this world his soul was bound
In bitter bonds of greed.
In courts of Pain
Shall the Judgment be.

And many men drew near to me —
Each carried burning sod,
May God have pity on their souls,
They'd moved the landmarks in the wood.
In affliction's courts
Shall the Judgment be.

6. Olaf Åsteson next observes the fiery realms where the damned carry burning coals and children who cursed their parents walk on coals of fire.

Children came up along the ways
Walking on coals of fire —
May God have mercy on their souls
Who cursed their parents dear,
In Courts of Pain
Shall the Judgment be.

To the House of Shame I made my way
Where witches together crowded,
I saw them standing in crimson blood
With such evil were they loaded.
In Brokksvalin
Shall the Judgment be.

Such heat there burns in the depths of Hell!
A heat no man can imagine.
They bended over their cauldron well
And flung a sinner's body in.
In Brokksvalin
Shall the Judgment be.

The hunt came faring out of the North
    Riding along so quick and crack —
And right in the front rode grim Grey-beard
    Leading his hell-wild hunting pack.
        In Brokksvalin
        Shall the Judgment be.

The hunt came faring out of the North
    The blackest hunt methinks of all
And right in the front rode grim Grey-beard
    On a stallion black as a pall.
        In Brokksvalin
        Shall the Judgment be.

Then came the faring out of the South
　　And all that came were quiet and blest,
For now in the front St Michael rode
　　And at his side was Jesus Christ.
　　　　In Brokksvalin
　　　　Shall the Judgment be.

From southwards they came, and more and more
　　Most noble was the pageant now —
'Twas Michael of Souls rode on before
　　And his horse was whiter than snow.
　　　　In Brokksvalin
　　　　Shall the Judgment be.

Out of the south came riding the host
　　It seemed in never-ending bands,
The Holy Michael of Souls foremost,
　　Who carried healing in his hands.
　　　　In Brokksvalin
　　　　Shall the Judgment be.

7. The Devilish hordes sweeping down from the North, with old greybeard at their head, are driving the lost souls before them.

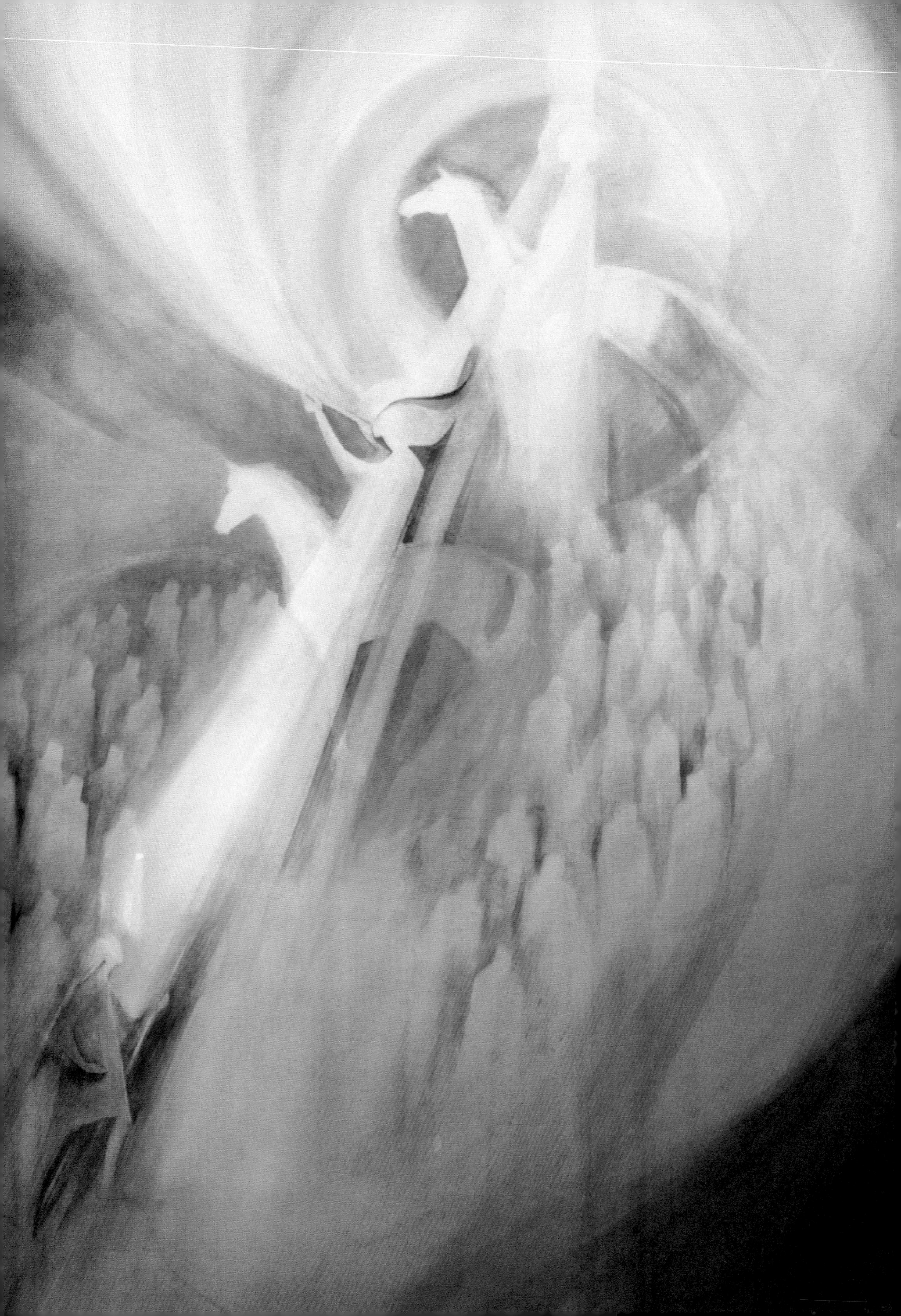

Michael the Lord of Souls it was then
    Who blew long and loud on his horn,
Calling to all the souls to go in
    To the Judgment so dread and lorn.
        In courts of Pain
        Shall the Judgment be.

See how the sinful souls are a-shake
    Like the aspen leaves blown by the wind,
And never a single soul is there
    But weeping knows well it has sinned.
        In affliction's courts
        Shall the Judgment be.

8. Coming now from the South, Olaf sees the noble host of the quiet and blessed souls, with the mounted Archangel Michael sounding his horn, calling them to judgment, accompanied by the shining figure of Christ.

It was St Michael, holy and good
Who ever in his balance cast
The trembling souls that around his stood
And bore them to Jesus at last.
In Brokksvalin
Shall the Judgment be.

Blessed is he who here on Earth
Gives shoes unto the poor,
For he may walk the thorny heath
With naked feet and sure.
The tongue shall speak
And truth attest on Judgment Day.

Blessed is he who in this world
Gives bread unto the poor
He has no fear in spirit-land
When hungry hounds draw near.
The tongue shall speak
And truth attest on Judgment Day.

9. Olaf now beholds the majestic figure of Michael, weighing all souls in his scales. Through him, light streams in radiance upon the redeemed.

Blessed is he who here on Earth
Shall give the poor his corn,
He will not fear on Gjaller Bridge
The Bull's sharp-thrusting horn.
The tongue shall speak
And truth attest on Judgment Day.

Blessed is he who here on Earth
His clothes the naked brings,
He need not fear in the other world
The dreadful frozen springs.
The tongue shall speak
And truth attest on Judgment Day.

The aged man and young men too
Have listened and attended
To his, to Olaf Åsteson
Whose Dream-song now is ended.
Rise up, thou Olaf Åsteson
Thou hast been so long-a-sleeping!

10. Olaf glimpses the realms beyond our world, where the stages of moving through the planetary spheres are experienced in life after death.